P9-CLS-595

The Ultimate Guide to Grandmas & Grandpas!

by Sally Lloyd-Jones

illustrated by Michael Emberley

HarperCollins*Publishers*

The Ultimate Guide to Grandmas and Grandpas! Text copyright © 2008 by Sally Lloyd-Jones Illustrations copyright © 2008 by Michael Emberley Manufactured in China. All rights reserved. No part of this book may be used or reproduced in any manner whatsoever without written permission except in the case of brief quotations embodied in critical articles and reviews. For information address HarperCollins Children's Books, a division of HarperCollins Publishers, 10 East 53rd Street, New York, NY 10022. www.harpercollinschildrens.com Library of Congress Cataloging-in-Publication Data Lloyd-Jones, Sally, 1960- The ultimate guide to grandmas and grandpas! / by Sally Lloyd-Jones ; illustrated by Michael Emberley. — 1st ed. p. cm. Summary: Provides insights into making your grandparents happy, from singing and dancing for them to letting them give you special treats and presents. ISBN 978-0-06-075687-1 (trade bdg.) ISBN 978-0-06-075688-8 (lib. bdg.) [1. Grandparent and child—Fiction. 2. Family life—Fiction.] I. Emberley, Michael, ill. II. Title. PZ7.J258Ult 2008 2007020880 [E]—dc22 CIP AC Typography by Allison Limbacher 09 10 11 12 13 SCP 10 9 8 7 6 5 ❖ First Edition

For Harry and his granny with love
—S.L-J.

To Adrian, for training her grandma
and grandpa so well
—M.E.

When you have a grandma

or a grandpa,

you need to **sing** to them

and **dance** for them

and **paint** lovely pictures for them.

You need to scream and run away when they pretend to be a monster. And let them chase you around the backyard.

When you have a grandma or a grandpa,

you need to
hold their hand
when they cross
the street.

And help them park the car.

When it's nice outside,
it's good to take
your grandma and
grandpa on picnics

and show them your running …

and your swimming.

(But you must be able to see them
all the time in case they run off.)

You need to teach your grandma football,
let her score touchdowns, and then shout,

"Good job,
Grandma!"

47
47

It's important to let your grandpa have some of your ice cream, and let him build you big sand castles like when he was a boy. (You have to let him sit in them.)

And then you need to knock them over so he can do it again.

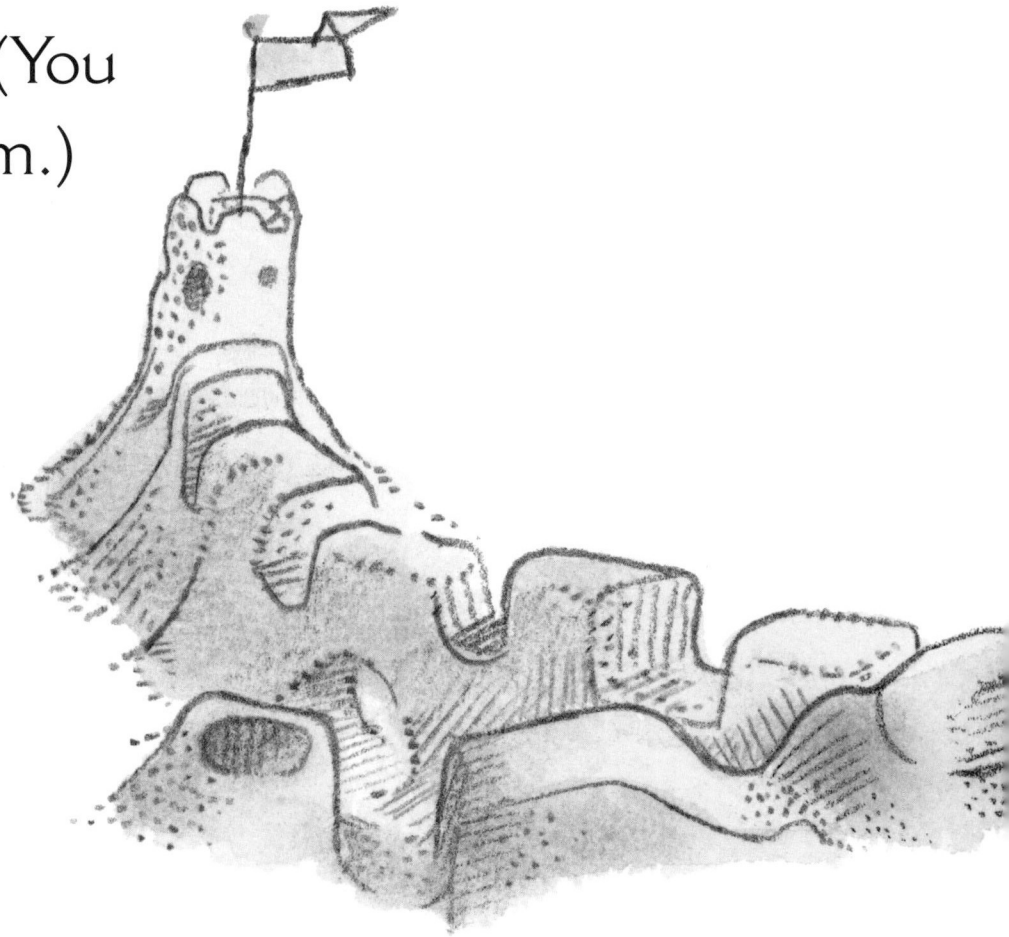

You need to make sure your grandma and grandpa have their naps when they're tired.

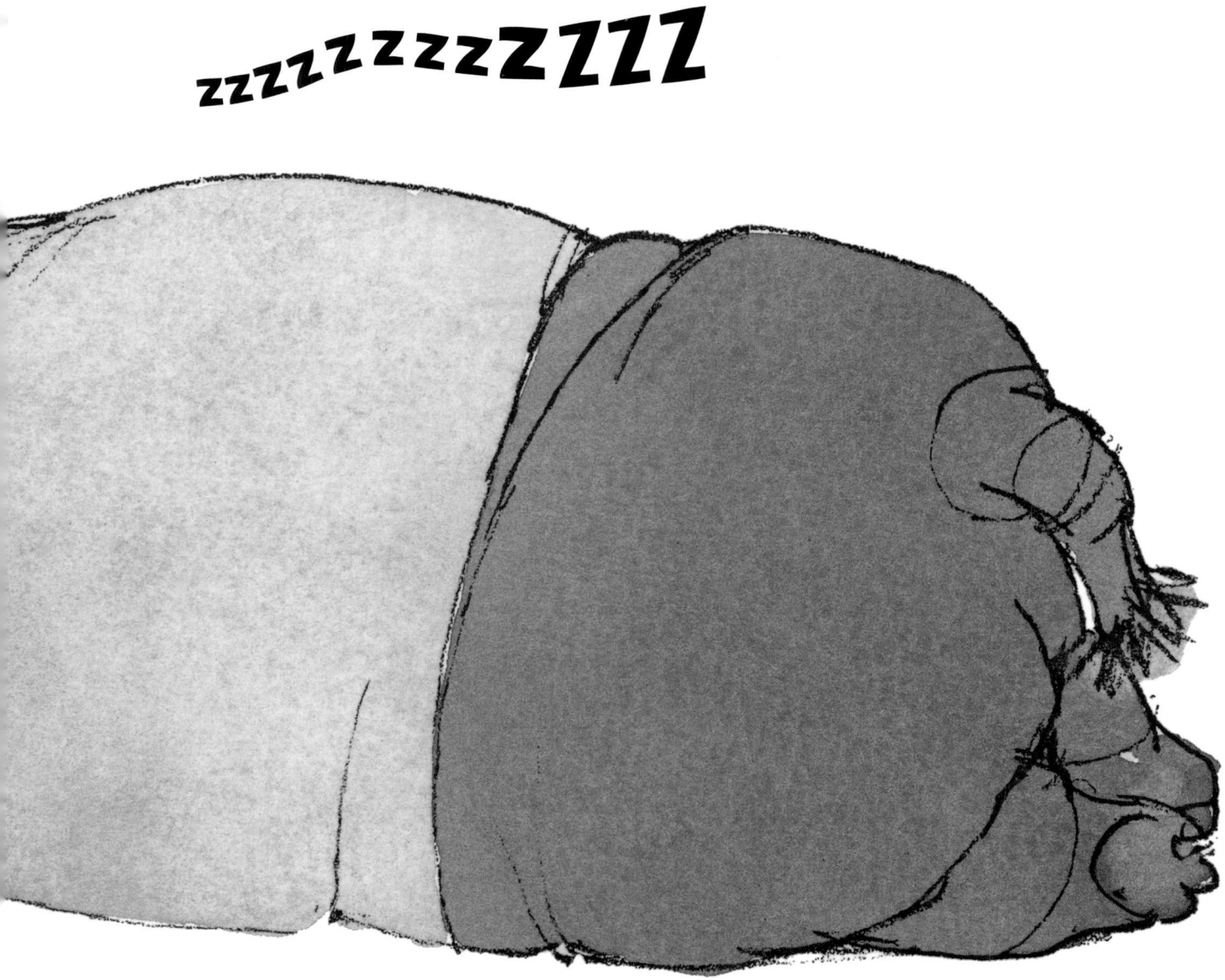

(Sometimes you have to take a nap with them so they're not the only ones.)

And if they're sick, you must let them borrow your special blanket.

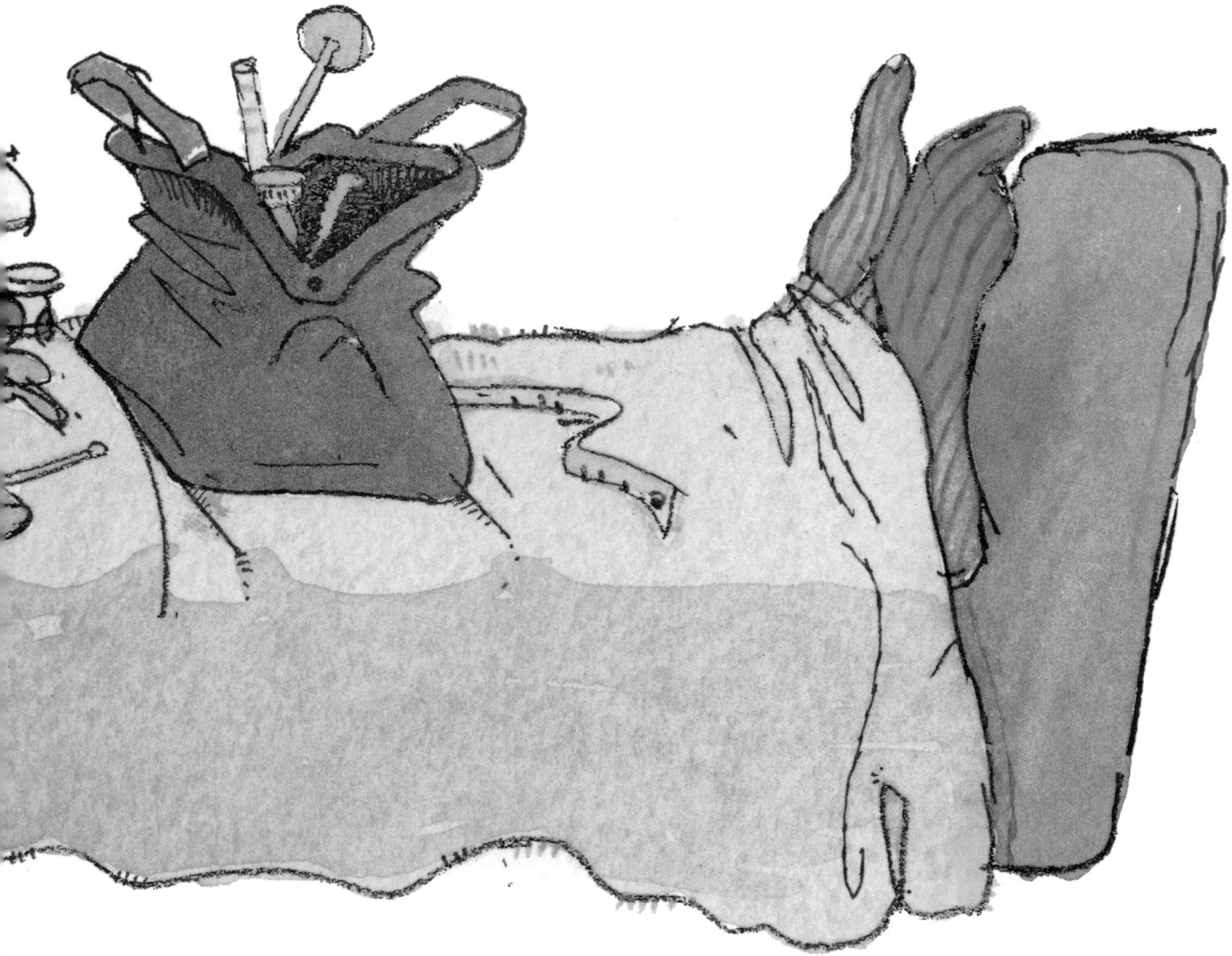

When you have a grandma or a grandpa,
you need to always play with them.

And sometimes let them win.

You need to always love their dinners and
eat them up and always ask for more.
And let them give you special treats
you're not allowed at home.

You must always let them give you presents.
And keep you up too late.

You must sit in your grandpa's lap so he can practice his reading on you.

And before you go to sleep, you need to listen to your grandma's stories about Black Beard and Pirates and *Danger* on the High Seas.

When you have a grandma or a grandpa,
you need to let them make you things.
And tell you secrets about how
naughty your mommy was
when she was little.

LONG NECK

And when they throw you up in the sky, a good thing to shout is,

(And then you let them tickle you.)

And, when you wave good-bye, a
good thing to say is, "Au revoir!"
(Which means you'll come back soon.)

But mostly, when you have
a grandma or a grandpa,

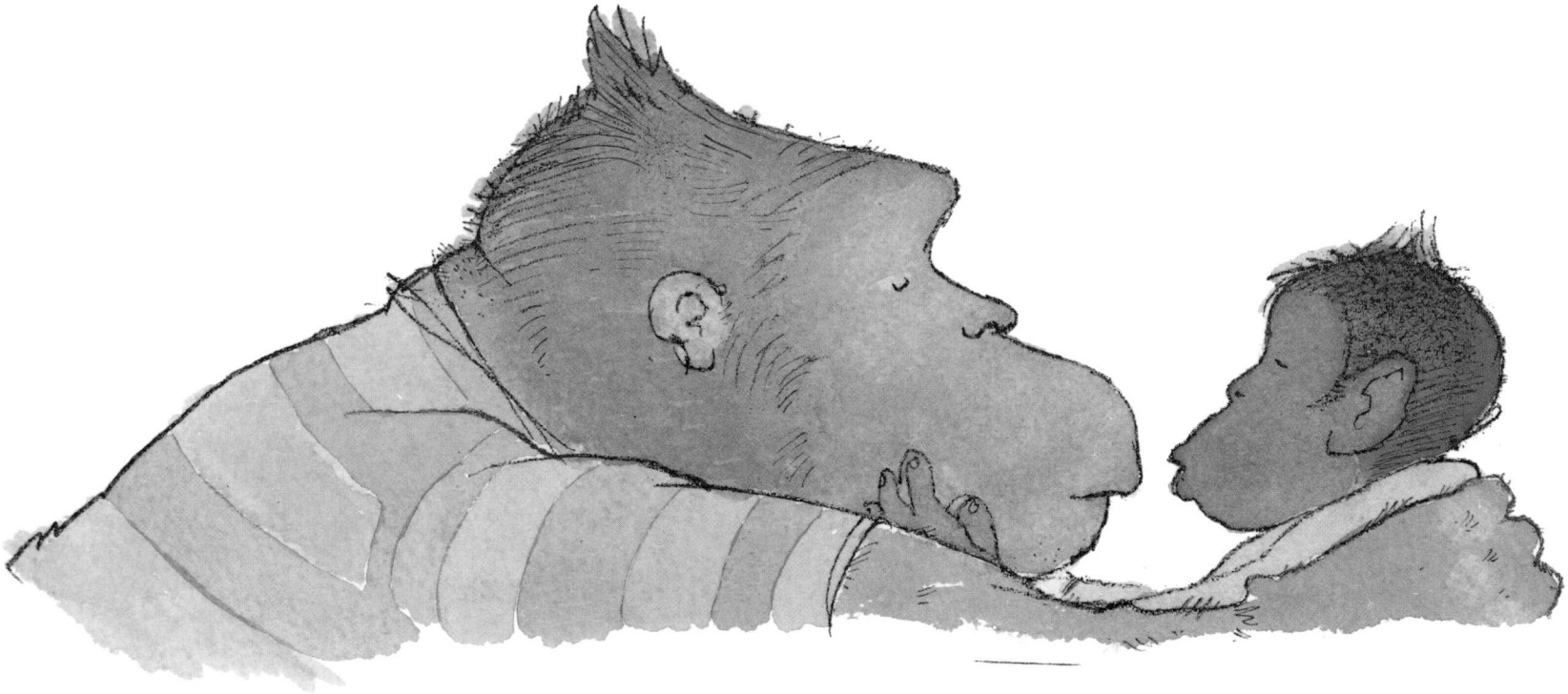

you need to **kiss** them.

And, when you wave good-bye, a
good thing to say is, "Au revoir!"
(Which means you'll come back soon.)

But mostly, when you have
a grandma or a grandpa,

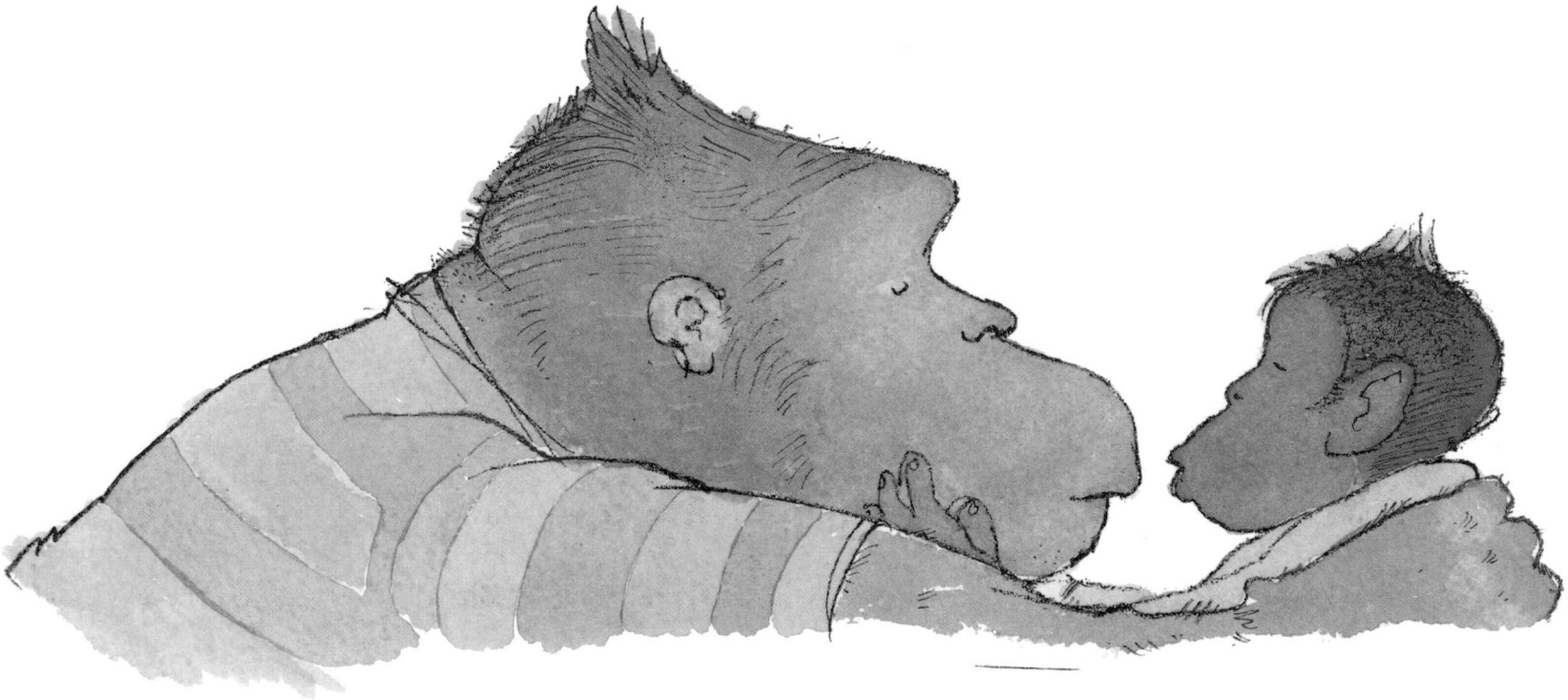

you need to **kiss** them.

And **hug** them.

And always
love them.

Because that's what grandmas and grandpas like best in all the world.